THE POPCORN BOOK

Tomie de Paola

THE POPCORN BOOK

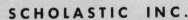

SCHOLASTIC INC.
NEW YORK · TORONTO · LONDON · AUCKLAND · SYDNEY · TOKYO

FOR FLORENCE NESCI,
*who taught me how
to pop the best popcorn
in the whole wide world*

ISBN 0-590-03142-2

12 11 10 9 8 7 6 5   3 4 5 6 7/8

Printed in the U.S.A.   07

"Popcorn was discovered by the Indian people
in the Americas many thousands of years ago.

"One of the first sights Columbus saw
in the New World was the Indians in San Salvador
selling popcorn and wearing it as jewelry."

FIRST, I HEAT UP THE PAN.

"But popcorn is even older than that.
In a bat cave in New Mexico, archeologists found
some popped corn that was 5,600 years old."

"And 1,000-year-old popcorn kernels were found in Peru that could still be popped."

"The Indian people of the Americas
had many different ways to pop popcorn.
"One way was to put an ear of corn on a stick
and hold it over a fire.

"But many kernels were lost in the fire
with this method."

"Another way was to throw the kernels right into the fire by the handful.

"The popcorn popped out all over the place, so there was a lot of bending and running around to gather it up."

"In 1612, French explorers saw some
Iroquois people popping corn in clay pots.

"They would fill the pots with hot sand,
throw in some popcorn, and stir it with a stick.
"When the corn popped, it came to the top
of the sand and was easy to get."

"The Iroquois people were fond of popcorn soup."

"The Algonkians who came to the first Thanksgiving dinner even brought some popcorn in a deerskin pouch.

"The colonists liked it so much that they served popped corn for breakfast with cream poured on it."

"Popcorn pops because the heart of the kernel
is moist and pulpy and surrounded
by a hard starch shell.

"When the kernel is heated,
the moisture turns to steam
and the heart gets bigger until
the shell bursts with a 'pop.'"

"The Indian people had a legend that inside
each kernel of popcorn lived a little demon.
When his house was heated,
he got so mad that he blew up."

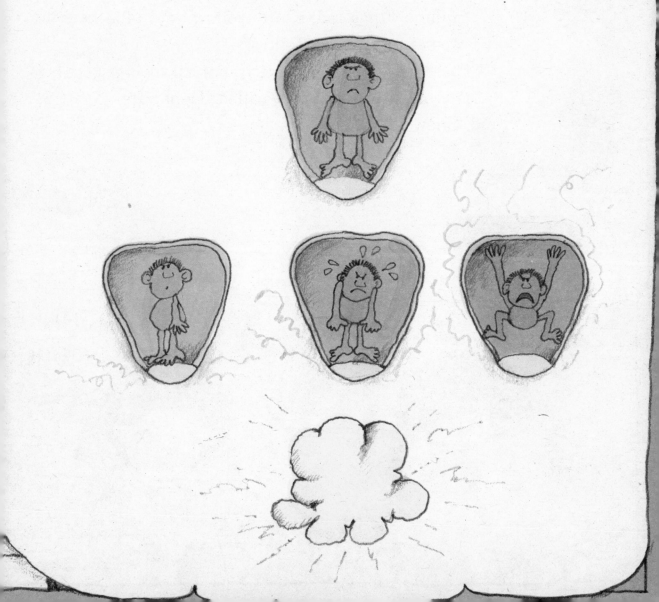

"There are different kinds of popcorn:
White hull-less and yellow hull-less are the ones
most commonly sold in stores.

"The smallest type is called 'strawberry' because
it has red kernels and the ears look like strawberries.

" 'Rainbow' has red, white, yellow, and blue kernels.
It is sometimes called 'Calico.'

"There is black popcorn, too, but all of it pops white.

"The biggest kernels are called 'Dynamite'
and 'Snow Puff.' "

SHAKE-
SHAKE-
SHAKE-

"After popcorn is popped, most people
like to put melted butter and salt on it.

"But if salt is put in the pan
before the kernels are popped,
it makes the popcorn tough."

"There are many stories about popcorn.
One of the funniest and best-known
comes from America's Midwest.

One summer, it was so hot and dry
that all the popcorn in the fields
began to pop.

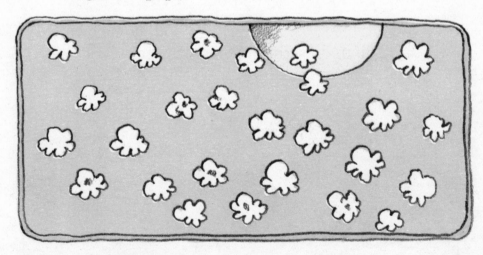

In no time at all, the sky was filled
with flying popcorn.

It looked so much like a blizzard,
everyone put on mittens and scarves
and got out the snow shovels."

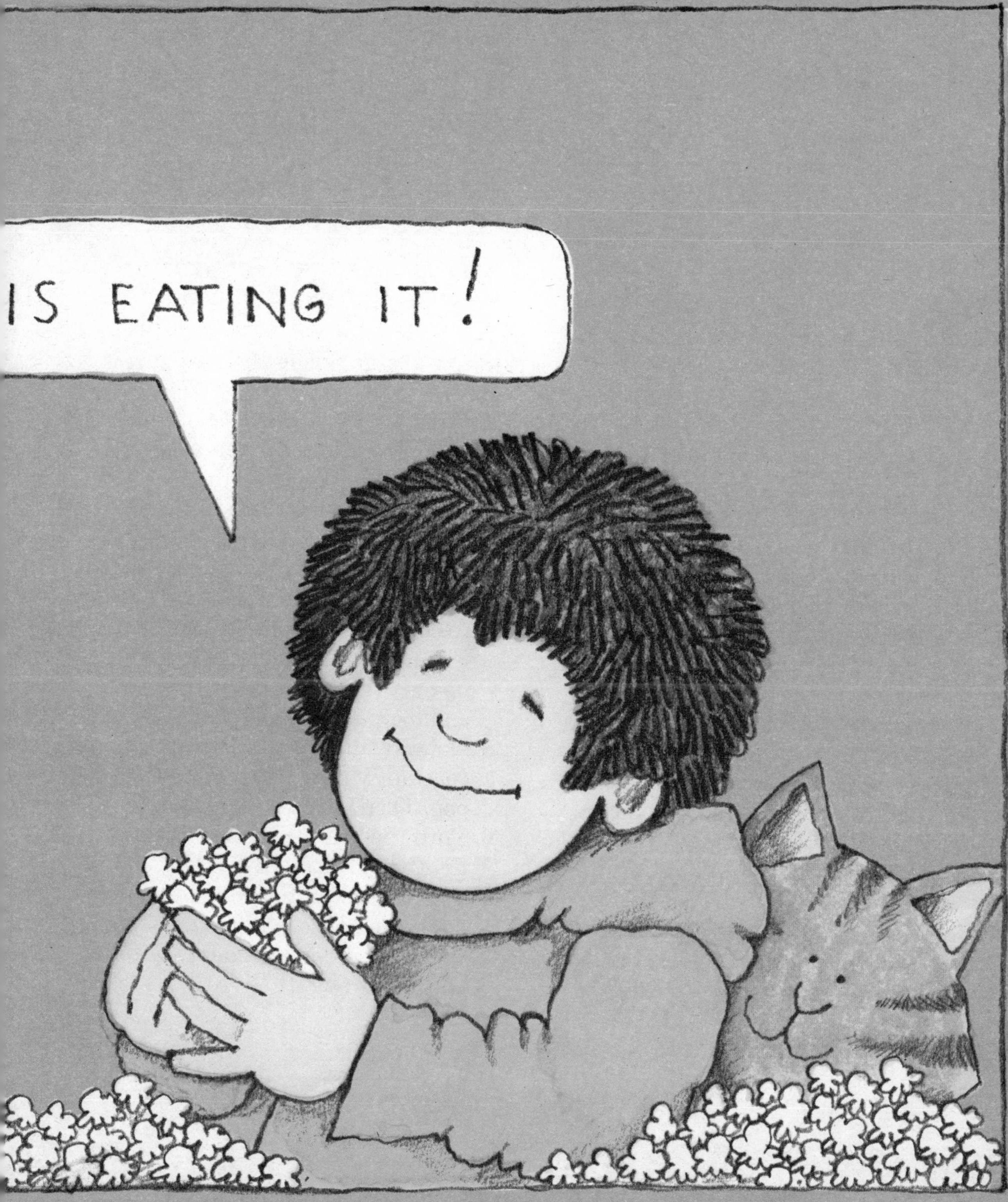
IS EATING IT!

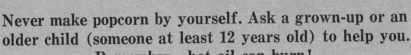

TWO TERRIFIC WAYS TO POP CORN

Never make popcorn by yourself. Ask a grown-up or an older child (someone at least 12 years old) to help you. Remember — hot oil can burn!

EVERYDAY WAY

1. Use a heavy 3-quart saucepan that has a cover.
2. Put the pan on the stove. Turn the heat on high for 2 minutes.
3. Pour ¼ cup of cooking oil into the hot pan. The oil should cover the bottom of the pan.
4. Turn the heat down a little. Add 3 or 4 kernels. They will sizzle in the hot oil and then pop.
5. When the 4 kernels pop, add more kernels — enough to cover the bottom of the pan. (Do not use more than ½ cup.)
6. Turn the heat to low and put the cover on the pan. Hold the cover tightly and shake the pan back and forth very fast.
7. When the popping stops, turn the heat off and take the pan away from the stove. Dump the popcorn into a bowl. Pour on some melted butter and sprinkle with salt.
8. Eat!

FRIDAY NIGHT POPCORN
Florence Nesci's recipe

1. Use a large skillet (frying pan) that has a cover.
2. Get a can of vegetable shortening (like Crisco). Scoop out a big spoonful and put it in the skillet.
3. Put the skillet on the stove and turn the heat on low.
4. When the shortening melts, pour in some popcorn kernels — just enough to cover the bottom of the skillet. The melted shortening should come up over the kernels. If it doesn't, add more shortening to the skillet.
5. Now stir the kernels. Stir constantly until 1 or 2 kernels pop. Then put the cover on.
6. Turn the heat up. Hold the cover tightly and shake the skillet. Shake it fast until the popping stops.
7. Pour the popcorn into a bowl and salt it. You don't need any butter.
8. Eat and enjoy it!

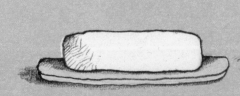